Teresa Ro
Throush Fait
possuble

cal nomain

STEPPING
TO THE SIDE

MW00975641

STEPPING TO THE SIDE

CARL MORRISON

TATE PUBLISHING
AND ENTERPRISES, LLC

Published by Tate Publishing & Enterprises, LLC
127 E. Trade Center Terrace | Mustang, Oklahoma 73064 USA
1.888.361.9473 | www.tatepublishing.com

Tate Publishing is committed to excellence in the publishing industry. The company reflects the philosophy established by the founders, based on Psalm 68:11,
"The Lord gave the word and great was the company of those who published it."

Book design copyright © 2016 by Tate Publishing, LLC. All rights reserved.
Cover design by Dante Rey Redido
Interior design by Shieldon Alcasid

Published in the United States of America

ISBN: 978-1-68270-770-8
1. Fiction / Religious
2. Fiction / Christian / General
16.01.26

Contents

1

A Battle Before Us

"THIS JUST IN: Today, Senator John Daniels has brought a bill before Congress to erase the tax exemptions of all religious organizations as well as nonprofit groups, and by doing so, it could almost pay off over half of the national debt.

Senator Daniels's saying that taxing religious organizations and nonprofit groups is an untapped sources of revenue that our country can use by making these organizations pay taxes on offerings and other means they get supported by.

"However, most, if not all, of the senators from the Bible belt have stood up and simply said one word in one voice. That word being *no*. They said it as if it had been practiced, but the bill had been kept so secret in its writing until now.

"Senator Henry Blake from Missouri said this was an outright attack on the Bible belt, and he also said he took it personally and that such a bill should not even be considered.

"Senator Daniels fired back, asking why he did not wish for states in the Bible belt to pay their fair share."

"Senator, Blake returned by saying that they should instead look at the useless spending that could be cut from the budget instead of forcing these groups and organizations to pay taxes on gifts given such as love offerings as well as tithes to churches, which up until last year was tax deductible.

"In other news…"

Jeff could not believe his ears he then turned the radio off and turned to Mike. "You know, Mike, we need to do something. This stuff is just the start of it."

"You're such a doomsdayer. I think they should start paying taxes. All they are doing is promoting the sale of an ancient book no one believes in any more. It's just a fairytale, right?"

"It's everywhere. Look here, in the paper they are given concert tickets away for Bibles."

"I mean it's like the nineties where you traded hand guns for tickets and sometimes gift cards. Me personally I would prefer to keep my gun."

"Mike, you're so lost. I wish you would listen to me and see what's going on here. Jesus is coming soon, and you're not ready. I pray one day before it's too late, you find Christ."

"Oh, I keep forgetting you believe in that garbage."

"It's not garbage, my friend. It's fact."

"Look, you could get me to believe in the great god of the talking hotdog before I would believe in the God you're talking about."

"You know, Jeff, your business has already taken a hit because of your so-called beliefs. You should reconsider letting everyone know you're a Christian. Remember what the LGBT did to you because you would not support them and told them how you believed and you would not support something like that because in your eyes it's wrong?"

"I did not lose that much business because people know Christians keep their word. The Lord took care of me during that time, and I got a bigger contract from a logo company. Mike, I am proud of who I am and who I trust as my Lord and Savior. My whole family trusts the Lord, and I know where I'm going and where my family is going when they die."

"So you're telling me that if someone told you they would kill your kid if you did not deny Christ, you would say, 'Go ahead, I know where he is going'?"

"Yes. For my kids are responsible for their own souls as I am mine. When they took Christ into their hearts, they became responsible for their relationship to the Lord. Though they still need guidance from me, they are the ones who answer to Christ. When I meet the Lord, I can only answer for myself no one else."

"That's a little harsh."

"It may sound that way, but it's the only way."

"Yes, but your own family…"

"Look at it this way. You get a traffic ticket. Do you let your dad take responsibility for it?"

"No, that's different."

"How so?"

"Uh, um, well, it just is."

"Is that the best answer you have?"

"You know there is one, I just can't explain it. Your Jesus did that for you, did he not?"

"Yes, he did, and we all should be glad and grateful for that fact, but he is the only one who can do that for us."

"Yes, but are we not all going to burn anyway according to your Bible. It says something like 'the wages of sin is death.'"

"Yes, but in John 3:16, Jesus sais, 'Whosoever believes in me shall not perish but have everlasting life. Thus those that trust Christ are saved because they give their all to the Lord even though sometimes we stumble, we know we're wrong. We repent of our sins and beg—not ask, but beg—for forgiveness."

"You have an answer for every thing, don't you?"

2

Meet Jane

J ANE HAS FIERY red hair. She was your typical seventeen-year-old girl.

She was a whiz with animation, very talented with music, and skillful with anything she put her mind to.

Jane's friends had one hang-up about her, but since she was such a good person, they overlooked it. You see, Jane seemed to think every conversation she had always seemed to go back to God and Christ, which seemed to annoy her friends, but on the same note, it also amazed her friends how much she loved and trusted the Lord.

Jane was also very active in most school clubs, like Beta club, debate club, the band, and the church youth choir.

She was great with the trumpet; she could really make it sing on its own. When she picked it up, one could smile because Jane was playing it.

Her animation was no different; she had done some stuff for her church, and some of it had gone throughout the Baptist convention.

Some of it was used for the Upward basket program, thanks to her brother, who is a wizard when it came to computers and audio visual tricks as well.

They were of course your typical siblings; sometimes they fight, but when they were not fighting, they deeply cared about one another. They always seemed to be there when they needed each other.

Now don't get me wrong here; they had their problems and were not perfect. They had a few hang-ups on their own, but both asked God for help, both knew one thing, and that was sometimes God says no.

Kim woke Jane from falling asleep in class. "Jane, Jane, wake up. Class is almost over."

Jane moaned and sounded annoyed. "Uh, I did all this already."

"I did this yesterday for homework, I know it."

Mr. Ren chimed in, "Well, young lady, can you answer this question? Do it on the board."

"Fine, but if I get it right, don't bother me until class is done with."

She then smiled, looked at the problem, and started writing the answer on the board as if she had hung on to every word the teacher had said.

"There you go. Gosh, please give me something complicated. This is too easy."

"Jane, you know this is advanced college-level trigonometry, right?"

"I guess so. That's what my books says anyway."

Jane sat back down, opened her notebook, and started drawing in anime style her teacher. He is dressed as a hero, and the problem on the board seemed to be attacking him while he had an extreme look on his face.

Mr. Ren looked over the board and could find no fault with her formula as to how she solved the complicated problem.

He then smiled.

"You're right, young lady. But please stop being so sarcastic about how smart you are. How did you know the answer?"

"Easy. I study."

"Now please show a little respect."

"I'm sorry, I was just trying to wake these other zombies so they could learn it. Really, I was helping you out."

She then batted her green eyes and tossed her flaming red hair back as if she was Miss Little Innocent.

Both knew it was all an act so the kids would wake up and pay attention.

With Jane's sarcasm and slight disturbance, the kids would wake up and see Jane solve the problem. Kim Sands was also in on the whole ploy because Jane was really that smart, but her attitude was nothing like how she acted in trig class.

After class, she placed the picture on his desk.

"Very funny, Jane. I will post it right here."

They both laughed.

Most kids knew it was an act because of who was doing it: Jane.

"Jane, you know every one knows this is just a show, don't you?"

"Of course, I do since we do this when we cover something every one has given up on."

"It gives them hope that if I can do it, maybe, just maybe, they can do it too. Just like Christ gives me hope."

"Jane, please, does everything have to go back to God when we talk?"

"Speaking of such, have you heard about the new teacher who is teaching world civilization?"

"I don't think he will last if he tries to teach the big bang theory and evolution as well."

"I'm not going to take a test on those things. I simply can't do that."

"Are you serious? You're willing to mess up your GPA over something like that?"

"Yup."

Jane looked Kim in the eyes, and she knew she was serious. Kim knew that look, which meant there was no way she would change her mind about the issue. She was not going to back down, grade point average or not. "Well, let's not make up our minds until we meet him. He may not even teach it."

"True, but I will not take the test if he does. The only thing I will do is put my name on it."

Kim and Jane walked into Mr. Parks's class just as he finished placing small booklets on each desk.

The final bell rang for class to start.

"Hello, class. I'm Mr. Tim Parks, and from here on out, I will be your world civilization instructor."

"Now on your desk is a summary of what we will be learning for the next nine weeks. Now to answer a few unasked questions. Ms. Bonner will not be back due to her illness. As you may already know, she has cancer, and it has gotten to the point she can no longer teach. So let's keep her in our thoughts."

Jane flipped through the small booklet, and it did not take her long to see what she was looking for. There it was, the big bang theory. Jane raised her hand.

"Yes, and you are?"

"I'm Jane Harrper, and I have a question."

"Then ask please."

"Why are you teaching something that no one has a clue about as far as mainstream science is concerned?"

"What are you talking about, Ms. Harrper?"

"The big bang and evolution. Both theories are so ridiculous it's laughable."

"No more laughable than what Christians tell how the world was created."

"Mr. Parks, most, if not all of us, are Christians here, and as far as it goes, something had to make the world, not something just blowing up and—*wam!*—a whole world with a complicated ecosystem. It had to be planned out."

"Miss Harrper, we could debate this until we are both blue in the face. However, if you don't do the work, you will fail this class, young lady."

Jane smiled that smile, the one that would leave you wondering if you won the argument or not.

"Okay, class, since Jane has said it, I will put it to you like this: if you don't do the work on this study, you will fail the nine weeks."

The class muttered.

"Okay, now turn your books to page 137."

Every one seemed to listen to the lesson, even Jane. Then the bell rang for class to end.

As Jane was about to leave class, Mr. Parks called her. "Jane, may I speak to you for a moment?"

"Sure, Mr. Parks."

"Look, I don't wish any trouble between us, but if you insist on disturbing my class with this attitude, I will have to have you removed from my class."

"Mr. Parks, if you kick me out of your class for stating how I believe and talk down to those that trust Christ, you're going to have a very empty classroom."

Jane then walked out of the room casually as if nothing had happened, and Mr. Parks was left wondering if he was going to have trouble out of her.

3

Meet Jason

JASON WAS VERY spoken on how he believed, and he was a genius in his own right—computers and audio-visual science of any kind. But he was not what you would call a geek. He was like most people, but when it came to God, there was only one way to go, and that was God's way.

"Mark, I heard that Mr. Parks is teaching evolution and the big bang theory."

"Yeah, and he told your sister if she makes too much of a fuss, he would kick her out of class," Mark said.

"You know, Mark, I will do the same thing, to tell you the truth. We should all do the same thing about this," Jason replied.

"Sort of a student protest, right?"

"Yup."

"Maybe he would get the message that this will not fly here."

"Does anyone know where he is from?"

"I heard he was from somewhere out west."

"Mark, do you think we can get every student to do this on the class work and test?"

"We can try. That's all we can do, but how far are you willing to go?"

"Until he is done teaching it."

"That's a lot of grades with zeros on them. I don't know how many will go along with it."

"This won't work without every one doing this."

"Jason, if you're serious, we will go along with you, but you know you're putting scholarships in danger, don't you?"

"What's more important, college or God?"

"Well, when you put it that way, I see your point."

"We will need time to get started."

"We don't have time. We need to get the word out. Jane will be down with this too."

"Yup, I think so."

"You know, since you're putting scholarships on the line, I think a lot of people will follow your example."

"Let's hope so, Mark."

4

The Plan

AFTER SCHOOL JASON and his friends met up with Jane and her friends at the church teen center where he told them about his idea.

The six of them got right to work, not doing their homework for Mr. Parks's class. It started at the teen center, but they ended up at the I-Net, an Internet cafe that was popular with most kids.

They got back lots of replies from all their friends willing to do it for as long as Jason and Jane both did it.

It was late, and they had finished reading the last of the replies and now knew everyone who were in Mr. Parks's class was on board with the silent protest.

Jason and Jane both wondered if they should tell their dad about what they were about to do.

They both agreed that they would simply wait and see what happened after tomorrow.

Jeff was watching TV.

"Hello, hello, hello! We have free cell phones to give away for those who give up their family Bibles! You will receive the new Galaxy 34 smartphone just for bringing us your family Bible. Don't worry if you don't have a family Bible. Bring two Bibles of any type, and you will receive the new Galaxy 34 as well. All you have to do is bring it by WXKP Studio and receive your free phone.

"And now for the top stories in the news. New genders—that's right. There are now four gender classifications—male, female, and then you have male-female and female-male, which fall into the transgender area. Also, for those identifying as transgender instead of having that as an identity of gender displacement now has a gender of their own.

"Some mainstream stores are already making way for the new genders by adding a third bathroom with the transgender symbol, a combination of the male and female symbols, on the door.

"Clothing manufacturers and designers have also gotten into the act. Due to the male body being somewhat bigger than the female body, clothing designers have started designing clothes that would make the male-girl look more feminine without looking odd if wearing women's clothing.

"On to the world news: Israel is talking about leaving the United Nations because of what they are calling mistreatment from other nations for going along with the sanctions that England has placed on them because they defended themselves from Iran with a decisive counterattack that ended up taking lives of some civilians.

"Jack Norman, representative for the United States, said that they support the sanctions because of the amount of loss of life from their counterstrike. The representative from Israel said that the war between them and Iran is just that, a war, and there will be civilian casualties on both sides."

Jeff sat there in his easy chair. The news no longer shocked him; he simply prayed and lived his life. With the news and what was happening around him, he knew God was coming and coming soon.

Jason came into the living room. "Dad, can I ask you a question?"

"Sure, son, what is it?"

"Well, not sure how to put this, but let's say I have this friend, and he sees something wrong, and it's part of the rules at school, but it's so wrong you simply can't do it. You simply can't bring yourself to do this, so you decide not to do this. But it could cost you big time. Would you stand up and still say it's wrong?"

"Jason, what does this deal with?"

Jason could never keep a secret from his dad, so he did not even try to hide what was on his mind.

"Well, it's our new teacher. He is planning on teaching about evolution and about creation, you know, the big bang, and I simply can't bring myself to study it or take the test or whatever he gives out.

"I know in the Bible it says God created the heavens and the earth, and so since I feel what is being taught is so wrong, I got some friends together, and we planned that we are not going to participate in class while he is teaching it. I know it's going to hurt my GPA, but it's a stand I feel I must take."

Jeff looked at his son with thoughtful look on his face. "Son, every man must take his stand in the world it's a part of growing up. If you feel you should make this stand whether you do this alone or with a group, it's still the stand you must make, and when you take a stand for God, God will stand by you.

"This is part of being a servant of Christ. We as Christians need to take stands even when it could cost us everything. We need to take that stand. We do not need to simply sit quietly while the rest of the world goes down a path that they don't need to. Also, as it is a godless path, we should stand up and be heard.

"Son, do what you think you should do, and I will stand behind you. Not only that, God will stand behind you as well. By the way how many are doing this?"

Jason looked his dad in the eyes and said, "Everyone who has Mr. Parks as a teacher."

5

The Stand

THE NEXT MORNING, both Jason and his sister's phones were a flurry of text messages from others who had agreed to the plan.

It was fourth period. Jason and his best friend, Mark, walked into class as did everyone else. They gave Jason a nod, letting him know they were going to do it.

"Good morning, class. I had given you some homework yesterday. Would you please pass that to the front."

As agreed, they turned in their work with verse Genesis 1: 1–31 instead of the assigned work. As agreed, they had written Genesis 1:1–31 for their home work instead of what they were suppose to have done.

Mr. Parks did not look at the papers right away. He went on showing how evolution of man occurred.

From the primate stage up to modern man, Mr. Parks showed the chart of progression of how man developed into what he is now.

All the students appeared to be taking notes, but none of them were doing that. They were writing Bible verses dealing with creation and the creation of man instead of the things Mr. Parks was teaching.

After he had finished teaching today's lesson, he sat down to review the work the kids had done.

When he looked at the first one, it was Jason's paper, and on it was written the entire first chapter of Genesis, word for word. He looked up from the paper and glared at Jason; then he looked at the second and the fifth. His face was getting redder and redder with anger.

He then stood up. "Okay, class, give me what you have written for notes. I want to see them."

Jason's notes was chapter 1 of the book of Genesis. He glared at Jason.

His anger seemed to grow as he looked at each student's notes, but somehow he managed to contain his anger and kept himself from lashing out.

"Okay, students, I have no trouble failing each and every one of you, so if you continue with this and support this fairytale of how the earth was made, I will have no choice but to fail each and every one of you."

Mr. Parks's day was full of the same thing and the same verses, and none of them wrote down the notes; instead they wrote the entire first chapter of Genesis as notes.

The day was over, and Mr. Parks found out that Jane and Jason had started the protest; however, no one was called to the office, but there was always tomorrow.

Jason and Jane were home; it was around seven when the doorbell rang.

Jason answered the door. "Hi, Mr. Parks, what are you doing here?"

"As if you did not know, young man."

"Well, come on in. Let's talk about it."

"You and I have nothing further to discuss. It is now down to me and your father."

"Sure, have a seat. I will go get him."

The living room was done in a light-blue color. The sofa and loveseat were of royal blue. The solid wood curio held little figurines of eagles of various shapes and size. The room was not huge but comfortable.

Jeff was already halfway into the living room when Mr. Parks took a seat.

"Dad, this is Mr. Parks, the teacher I told you about."

"Oh yes. How are you today?"

"We need to have a talk about your son and your daughter."

He could see the {seering} anger in his eyes about the day's events.

"This is the homework they turned in today, and these are the notes they took." Mr. Parks handed the papers to Jeff, and he looked at them.

"I'm impressed, son. I did not know you could write from memory the first chapter of Genesis."

"Well, when you write it for homework, it tends to stick in your head," Jason replied.

"What's wrong with this, Mr. Parks?"

"This is not what I'm teaching, and I can't teach my class with this. All the students have done the same thing, and if this continues, I will see that both your son and daughter will be suspended. Let's see how they act when their GPAs drop {he said smugly}. How am I to teach this when the town teaches this fairytale."

"Mr. Parks, I'm sad to see you do not trust Christ, but you cannot fault an entire town for teaching their kids about God. If you do, you might as well move on instead of persecuting your students."

"Mr. Harpper, I came by to try and talk to you about your children, but it is obvious you are not going to listen to reason, so I will make it simple. Your kids don't do the work, they don't get the grades. They will fail my class all nine weeks of it."

"Well, Mr. Parks, you have made your point, but you need to look at all the papers your students gave you. They all say the same thing, don't they?"

After Mr. Parks left. "Okay, you two, if you're going to take a stand like this, you're going to have to stick to it no matter what. Now your faith will be tested because some will only remain strong for a short time. You two have to remain strong the entire time to show you will stand by your faith and not stop when it gets tough. It will get very difficult before this is over."

It was the middle of the week, and Mr. Parks had seen nothing but Bible verses about what they believed about how God created everything. As he was going through them, marking them with zeros as he had promised, he saw one with the right answers on it. Some were starting to cave in. Mr. Parks tried to control the smirk on his face when he saw three more. "Well, class, I see some of you are coming to your senses and are now doing your homework properly."

"Mr. Harrper, I think your protest of what I'm teaching is about to end, so why don't you just make it easy on yourself and start doing the work."

Jason stood up. "Sir, I will not do this because it goes against God's teachings, and I will never go against God."

Jane had seen the same thing in her class. It was almost test day; however, both Jane and Jason planned on being firm.

After school, they met at I-Net. When Wilma walked in.

"Jason, I'm sorry, but I do have to worry about my grades. I need to keep my C average. You know I'm not a great student. I just cant risk failing any class."

"I understand. Don't worry about it. You must do what you think is right for you."

Friday arrived, and it was test day.

Jason planned on answering the questions with Bible verses. He finished his test in what it would normally take him. He walked up to the desk and turned his test in, and no sooner did he do that, Mr. Parks glanced at it and then tossed it in the trash.

"Mr. Harrper, that is what I think of your fairytale and your answers on this test."

Jason turned and smiled at Mr. Parks. "Sir, I will pray for you."

Jeff was sitting in his office, wondering how Jane and Jason's fight was going. He decided to pray for them, for he knew it was going to get real tough real quick.

Jeff bowed his head.

Lord, I pray for my children, who have chosen to fight for how they believe in you and are standing against false teachings. I pray you give them strength and the courage to continue this fight until its end. Amen.

Jeff's thoughts were interrupted by the phone. It was Mike, one of his suppliers for his business.

"Mike, how is it going?"

"Well, Jeff, I got some new stuff you might be interested in."

"Yes, come on by, and I will take a look."

"Just one thing. I'm in a bit of a hurry, so can we do without you trying to convince me God is real today?"

"Sure, Mike, I have some things I need to do too."

Mike came by the office and showed a new line of T-shirts that were perfect for printing.

"These shirts are cheap and good, oh and one other thing, the owner is like you. He is a believer too. You know, Jeff, I'm starting to wonder if you might be right because I have run across a lot more people who trust Christ and truly believe wholeheartedly in God."

"Okay, since you started it, I can now tell you more right?"

"I knew you could not stand not saying something," Mike muttered.

"Since billions of dollars have been spent on temples, churches, and other things, not to mention the millions of people who trust Christ and have died for Christ, there has to be something to it, right?"

"So is Zeus real?"

"No, it's my thinking that some men who wanted to make some money created these gods and sold likenesses of them. Then it just turned into a lot of different religions. That was nonsense."

"So who's to say the same thing did not happen here?"

"Well, God has done so much. You can look at the world and know God is responsible for the creation of earth and mankind. Besides, there is no likeness of God anywhere. No one knows what he looks like, so how can someone sell a likeness of him when one of his ten commandments is not to worship images or statues of anyone? But everyone sees God but does not know it. He is all around us, in us. Well, he even created us. That's how I know he is real."

"You know, Jeff, you have given me something to think about even though you promised me you would not say anything."

"You started the conversation. Shall we get back to the samples now?"

6

Stand Strong

Jason and Jane came home a little down after seeing some of their friends who had committed to the cause fall to the side because of grades. Jeff had seen how upset both were and knew it was starting.

"Hey, you two, how did it go with Mr. Parks today?"

"We lost ten to fifteen in each class today. They started doing the work, and I'm afraid that we may lose more if we can't come up with a way to show people how serious it is."

"I told you there would be some that fall to the side, and I will also still support this as long as you are committed to this. You must not waver on this. For Christ did not waver from his commitment to us. You should try to do the same."

"Yes, sir."

Jason spoke up, "Dad, I can't stop after what I said today in class anyway."

"What did you say?"

"He asked me to give up on our protest since about ten students started doing the work. I said it was against God's teachings and I would not go against God."

Jane patted her brother on the back.

"Well said, little brother. Wish I had thought of that."

"Well, I have something that might cheer you two up."

"What is it?"

Both needing a major boost to get them back on track. "I got a letter today from your mother, and it says she will be home in a week. You can read it if you want."

Stacy was a career soldier and was a major in the tech division of the army. She was responsible for tracking incoming missiles and giving locations to fighters and the like to drop bombs and missiles so they would not hurt many civilians in the process. She also gave troops the locations of strongholds so they could coordinate their attack with other units.

The one thing that worried them all was how close to the front lines they were with their unit being nearly a hundred yards from the border of the North.

The next day was a gloomy day. It seemed to make everyone miserable. The clouds were gray, and it was almost windless. It was drizzling a bit, just enough to put everyone in an ill mood.

Jason met up with Mark before class with a few more of there friends.

"You know, Jason, we need to do something to get everyone's attention so they will get involved again because if we keep losing people, it will be a useless point with only a few making the stand."

"In the Bible, it says the road to hell is wide and smooth, but the road to God is rough and narrow. Even with a few, I think we might get some attention."

"Right now, we simply need God's grace and courage to get through this."

Jane and some of her friends had been coming up with ideas of getting attention to get everyone back on board.

"Jason, Mark is right. We do need to do something. Maybe we need more than just the students here. Maybe if we get attention and bring it on us, maybe we will get more support with this. Now all we need now is a good idea."

"How about after school we meet at the church teen center. Maybe we can get the student minister involved, and he might even have an idea or two."

"Sounds like a plan. Let's do this."

"We are going to lose more students today. They are putting their GPAs before God."

Sara was a spunky girl who seemed to be just as on fire for the lord as Jason and Jane; she was interested in the conversation that was going on. She also seemed as if she liked Jason a little more than friends. "What we need is something to prove how firm we are. I will try to think of something. Maybe I can help," she said.

Sara then skipped away, thinking this might get Jason interested in her.

As Jason and Jane walked down the halls, they saw students lower their heads in shame for falling to the side, but they had to take their future into consideration.

One of Jane's close friends stopped her in the hall. "Look, I can't keep getting zeros on my work. I did answer the questions the way Mr. Parks wanted, and I did the homework. It's been a week now, and I am ashamed, but my parents are not going along with this. They say my future has to come first."

Jane looked her in the eyes. "Madison, listen to me. Do you know what's going to happen tomorrow?"

"No."

"Who is to say Jesus won't come tonight and take us all to be judged? Where would you stand when God asks you why you left the fight? It's all about faith. It's all about God and standing up and saying in a loud voice, 'I serve God and Jesus is my Lord and savior.' That's why I won't leave the fight."

"Jane, you have to pick your battles you know you can win."

"No, you can't. God brought this battle for us to fight. You don't pick your battles when it comes to God. You stand firm with your faith and let God be the one who takes care of you, not some number that says you're smart."

Madison looked up and smiled. She reached in her bag and ripped up the homework she had done for Mr. Parks's class.

"You know what, you're right," a voice from behind them said.

He was a football player, and he ripped up his homework as well. Before they knew it, those who had fallen to the side for grades' sake were back on board.

The sound of ripping paper could be heard all the way down the hall.

With the sound of ripping paper still echoing in the halls, Mr. Parks came running into the faculty office.

"Mr. Hall, you're the principal. You must do something about this," Mr. Parks said angrily.

"What is wrong?"

"The first bell has not even rang out yet, but those two bratty kids have brought back their protest to full swing."

"I want those two expelled for disturbing the school discipline and being a major distraction in my class. I have one of those Harrpers in one of my early classes, and I know what he is going to have on his homework, more of that Bible garbage."

"Mr. Parks, I'm not only the principal of this school. I'm also a deacon of my church. What you are calling garbage is my holy book, and you should respect it as such! Now as far as disturbing the school is concerned, no, they are not. It is my understanding they are simply not doing the work in protest of what you are teaching."

"All this will end when you stop teaching it and move on to something else."

"The federal government requires us to teach it."

"Tim, do what you think you should, but I am not expelling or suspending anyone over this, so get that idea out of your head right now. This is a God-fearing town."

"This is outrageous. This is a church-and-state issue."

"Mr. Parks, this has nothing to do with church and state. It has to do with God and faith. No church has interfered and tried to turn the tide."

"Mr. Hall, I don't think the law will look at it that way."

"I think you're one man who is about to have a lot of problems on your hands if you make too much of a fuss about this here."

"The law is on my side, Mr. Hall. In my opinion, all of you act like it's the Dark Ages, believing in nonsense and superstition of something that is not real, and it's all based on a two-thousand-year-old book that should have been outlawed long ago, but the first amendment keeps it and your primitive faith in tact."

"Mr. Parks, if I were you, I would keep that to myself. Your class started two minutes ago. Don't you think you need to go teach?" Mr. Hall was coming close to losing his cool with Mr. Parks.

Mr. Parks left the office, and looking around, he did not see one piece of paper on the floor.

When he entered his classroom, all the students were in their seats, waiting for him to arrive.

"Good morning, class. Would you please pass your homework to the front."

No one passed any homework to the front at all. Not a single paper came forward. He looked at his class, tapped his chin, and sat behind his desk. "I see. Well, I can see we are going to have issues with this subject matter here, so I will give you a little incentive. I will give each of you who does today's work and the homework tonight a C average. You have until end of class to make up your mind." He said this in such a cold manner it was almost scary.

"Now, I'm going to start with evolution, and it's up to you what you do. We all started off as a single-cell organism, then we became fish. Then those fish came aground, and so about a million or two million years, we became monkeys, then on up to what we are now."

Mr. Parks saw no one was taking notes; they seemed to be staying firm on what they were doing and why they were doing it. *I have to find a way to beat this myth of God*, he thought to himself.

7

Mr. Parks

THE LAST BELL had rung to end the day, and Mr. Parks decided he needed to clear his head, so he went to the court square. It seemed peaceful and a good place to get his head together.

The fountain had the statue of a civil war hero and founder of the town. The fountain had a historical quote that had been rubbed off over time, making it difficult to read. All he could make out was "Through faith, all things are possible."

The quote only seemed to infuriate him more about what he was dealing with at school and how the students had went back to the protest of what he was teaching, so he decided to sit in the park and try not to read any more history texts on statues.

While sitting there, he noticed an elderly black man. He was wearing flannel shirt underneath an army jacket; lime-green suspenders held his old work pants. He was holding an old beat-up book bag of some sort and he also was holding a well-used Bible. He had a white beard that came just below his chin; it was a full beard starting at his sideburns. His boots were military issue.

The man looked like he had been through a lot in his life. Feeling somewhat sorry for what he must have been through, he decided to engage him in a conversation.

"Hi. Beautiful day today."

"Yes, God has given us a wonderful day today, not like this morning when he decided to let it rain a little to water his garden."

Tim started to leave.

"You're that new teacher that everyone is making a fuss about, the one teaching evolution. Sit down, let's talk about it. Besides you look like you could use a friend to talk to."

Tim turned around and noticed the bag the man had around his shoulder.

It had stamped on it: US Army Courier.

"You were an army courier, uh, Mr...."

"Call me Zeak."

"Well, Zeak, you were one of those unsung heroes in what war?"

"I was in the Korean War."

"Don't you mean *conflict*?"

"It was a war. I don't care what the government called it. It was a war when some one shoots at you with a cannon and when fighters drop bombs and people die for no good reason. It's a war."

"I lost half of my left hand to prove that point."

"I'm sorry. I did not mean to upset you. I will go."

"No, please stay. You must forgive this old man. I mean, I should have crusted over and died years ago, but I'm ninety-nine years old. I'm a bit stuck in my ways."

"I understand. My great-grandfather fought in that war. Where were you at during the war?"

"My HQ was in Seoul, but I was all over that place, I could not even start to tell you where all it was. One reason is I have been trying to forget all that since I got back in 1953. It's already this is 2034. A lot has happened since then."

"Yes, sir, it has. But things change, and people should change with it."

"What things do you think should change, Tim?"

"Well, sir, not to be disrespectful, but that book you're holding should be outlawed. It's full of hate."

Zeak laughed out loud. "Tim, this is one thing that should never change and should remain the same."

"Why is that?"

"This book is not full of hate. A book can't be filled with hate. Only the person reading it can be full of hate."

"The Bible is full of lessons: how to raise your kids, how to live life, what to do and how it do, and what not to do. Let me ask you a question. Now don't answer it right off. Think about it in a quiet place and then see where it stands."

"Okay, let's hear it."

"If evolution, the way science says it happened, occurred that way, where did shame come from?"

"Now, Tim, don't answer the question. Not yet. Simply think on it."

Tim did not truly understand the question that Zeak had asked him.

However, Tim was like most who did not want to hear something that an old person had to say, so he ignored it.

Jeff was sitting in his office when an idea hit him as a way to help keep the pressure on Mr. Parks so he might just reconsider teaching evolution.

8

Why Did You Help?

Basketball practice had ended, and Jason was leaving the gym when he saw someone getting beat up. It was Seth Parks, Mr. Parks's son.

He had heard about Seth. He dressed like a girl and never truly even showed interest in guys or girls, but he had been saying since day one that he had always thought of himself as a girl.

Jason shouted, "Hey! Hey! Stop that!"

"Jason, this is Seth, the sissy. He likes wearing girl's clothes."

"This is not what God would want. Just remember, Jesus ate with sinners of all kinds. He also talked and helped those who needed him. So what gave you the idea to beat up a young boy despite what he says? God made him a male, and he is lost. Instead of beating him up, you should

STEPPING TO THE SIDE

tell him about Christ. Does beating up a sixth grader make you feel good?"

"Well, no, it don't."

"Then why do it?"

"I don't know."

"Then get out of here!"

Seth was laying there with his arms still covering his head to protect himself from the blows he took.

"Seth, you okay?"

Seth wiped the tears from his eyes, and Jason could tell right off he was going to have a shiner. Jason saw some scrapes and cuts, but nothing serious. "Do you know why those idiots tried to hurt you?"

"Because I'm a girl on the inside and desire very much to be one on the outside."

"People like them should be hunted down and shot."

"That would make you no better than they are."

"Look, you need to think before you say something like that in front of people. Those guys already had you labeled a sissy. You should be more careful."

"Thanks. I will."

"Let's get you to your dad."

"Where is he?"

"He is in his office in the high school building." Seth tried to stand but fell back down.

"Ouch!" He had not noticed that he twisted his ankle when he fell.

"Let me help you. Then your dad can take it from there."

It took about five minutes to get up to Mr. Parks's office.

"Mr. Parks, I need your help. Please open the door."

"What is it?" Mr. Parks opened his office door and saw Jason helping an injured Seth.

"What happened? Who did this?"

"It was two tenth graders. I did not know them," Seth replied.

Mr. Parks looked at his son. He was not to bad off a twisted ankle and his other injuries were nothing serious.

"Thank you, Jason. But why did you help him? He is something your Bible detest."

"Mr. Parks, I helped him because it was not right no matter the reason they had, and Christ does not work that way. Jesus ate, spoke, and communed with sinners of all types, and he tried to show them the way to salvation."

"Jason, thank you for helping my son."

"Mr. Parks, I don't hate you. I don't hate anyone. We are simply on different sides of a disagreement, that's all. You must remember this: God hates the sin, not the sinner. Some people get that turned around sometimes. God also forgives as well because we all mess up sometimes."

"Why do you believe in God so much, and why this God?"

"Simple. God proves he is here all the time. Why, look at the clouds, look at the trees. No matter how you try to let science explain them, it comes back to what about the first one."

"Jason, what if there is no God and evolution is correct?"

Jason looked at him thoughtfully for a moment. "Mr. Parks, if a big bang occurred, how did the explosion occur, what caused the explosion, what caused the gases to appear, and what caused them to combine, not to mention where did it all of it come from?"

"Not to mention your science goes in a circle motion when it comes to that," Jason said.

"You know we both believe trust in the opposite end of the argument, and the sad thing is you have faith in science and I have faith in God."

Mr. Parks's anger about the entire day had resurfaced. He did his best to be respectful of Jason, who had stopped his son from being beaten to a pulp.

"I need to get Seth home so I can tend to his wounds. Thank you."

On the way home, Seth asked his dad something.

"Dad, if what Jason believes is full of hate, then why did he help me?"

"Son, I don't know. I really don't know."

Mr. Parks was trying to wrap his mind around Jason's kindness and did not understand the truth behind the Bible.

There were two famous preachers. One was Fred Phelps who did anything in his power, including slurs and messages of hate on posters, to speak against homosexuality. Then there was Billy Graham, who taught love and kindness to all of God's children.

"Son, that does not dismiss that what he is doing is wrong, causing trouble."

"What if he is right?"

"He is not right. I know this. I trust what I can see or read. How do you put faith in something you can't see or understand?"

The next day, Mr. Parks decided to talk to Jason about yesterday.

Jason was standing by his locker, looking for his fifth-period notebook.

"You dropped something, Jason." Mr. Parks picked up the notebook and handed it to Jason.

"Thanks."

"I wanted to thank you for helping Seth. If you stop this protest, I will give you an A minus, and we will end on good terms."

"Mr. Parks, I can't stop a battle that still needs to be fought."

"Why do you fight a battle every one has given up on nearly twenty years ago?"

"That's the problem. Every one is asleep. No one wants to fight for what they believe in. Well, me, I decided that I can't pick my battles that are in my path. I won't step around the fight and avoid it. That's why this country is in the shape it's in now. Why, Christianity is almost a dirty word now days. Even here, people turn their backs on this fight. It's not just about this issue. It's about all of them, and if God wants me to fight all of them with or without help, I will do it. I can't go on with life like it does not matter because it does."

"I have to admire your convictions, but I can't just stop teaching it. I do not believe in God, and I believe in science and what it shows me."

"Sir, think on this: science can only copy God's work, not match it in any way."

"The bell is about to ring. You need to get to class."

Mr. Parks walked in behind Jason. The class wondered what was going on. Had Jason given up the fight after all he had said and done, but they did not have to wait long to find out.

"Class, I know I'm going to regret this, but please pass your work to the front."

Jason handed his paper to the front like everyone else.

Once Mr. Parks got to Jason's paper, he looked it over. "No surprise here. None at all. More Bible verses. I'm going to discuss something that does deal with our world instead of our current subject because Jason here has made a point."

"Throughout our history, arguments have been won and lost on determination or the lack of. Both sides believe they are right. Both have those who support them like the people from that church in Kansas, Fred Phelps, the pastor of Westboro Baptist Church. The man has been dead for over twenty years, and he still has followers doing the same thing, being antigay through protest using slurs and other ways of making their point."

"The man used the same book as Jason does, but all that man did was blur what the book was truly about, and it had nothing to do with the hatefulness that Mr. Phelps has shown those people.

"Jason came up on my son who you all know is transgender, and he was getting beaten up by two bullies, and he stopped it and helped Seth back to my office. There are two totally different interpretation of the same book—one so far off the mark it negates the truth of the teachings no matter how false they may be or flawed the same book had a message of hate, and one message showed love and kindness. This is how lines of what someone stands for gets blurred.

"Wars in the world have often gotten started because of two parties taking away two entirely different messages from the exact same material word for word. In all conflicts, whether they be civil or war, the one thing you need to know is how the other party feels about what they are standing up for and why.

"However, if we did this as common sense dictates, then there would be no need for war or a government of any kind, but since we are human, there is not much we can do but decide what the people want and need. Now, class, this information we have discussed will be a bonus question, so treat this as part of your studies."

Jason wondered if Mr. Parks was starting to have a change of heart about the whole thing, but Mr. Parks had gotten half of the class back with the promise of a C from this point until the next grade came in then he would go from there.

9

The Fight Continues

PARENTS STARTED TO hear about the protest and how two of the smartest kids in school were leading the charge and were putting their academic life in jeopardy for their beliefs.

Some churches were just hearing about it, and Jeff was getting calls about it. They were wondering if there was something they could do to help with the fight.

What had been looked at as someone trying to gain attention, but that was not the case. It went deeper than that, and Jason and Jane were willing to put everything on the line just because that is how they were taught to believe by their parents, to trust Jesus completely with everything and to sacrifice it all for God. This was such a time to them.

The fight though was almost civil. No harsh words, no violence, just what Jason and the others who were still holding firm were doing.

However, some churches looked at this as some kids trying to get attention.

Even though it was the exact opposite, they stood up for what they believed and were willing to fight for it when others had simply stepped aside and let God take a backseat when the going got tough.

But this time, the fight was not going to go away because someone thought the battle was to tough and you had to pick your battles according to popular opinion. However, this was not going to be the case.

Jeff came home early to surprise the kids with his idea of how they could get others back into the fight.

He sat down and was watching the news as he waited on them.

"Welcome to Channel 10 News. Here is our first story. Since the dawn of social media, people have found dates on line and even carried on relationships and never met, but now a first many, where a marriage online and on a site called I-World, they have a virtual world where you can meet and even get married in a virtual church.

"These people who have never met or even spoken on the phone in person are having the world's first online wedding. Neither one has even seen a photo of each other or heard their voice in real time.

"The wedding will take place on I-World live as both their avatars walk down the aisle in a virtual church that they both have attended. All their dates took place in virtual Pleasant Town, where they met for the first time, and from there, the relationship grew to what it is today.

"We here at Channel 10 News wondered, was the wedding legal since all of it was done in a virtual world? We asked a lawyer this question, and here is his response."

The lawyer said, "As long as the person behind the avatar performing the ceremony is a registered justice of the peace or a minister of some sort with an established church, he can perform the wedding, and it can be recognized by the law as long as the marriage license is signed by both parties in a legal way and okayed by a notary republic."

"When we asked them about a real-time relationship, both of them said maybe someday when we asked and we're sorry we did now. What about kids? Their response was one disturbing way. The groom whom we call George said they plan on having real kids. He would send his semen to a doctor where his bride would have the procedure done."

"Both have said that children were a ways down the road. We will be right back after these messages."

"Welcome! Welcome to our new store completely outfitted with public restrooms for the two new genders and a great clothing line called Male-Girl, perfect for the female-male. Male-Girl also has a line of clothes for the male-female as well. So come on down to Wondermart!"

"Now for the weather."

"It's gonna be cold and real cold, so dig out those heavy coats because the temperature is going to dip below the thirty-degree mark, and the wind chill will make it feel like it's in the teens. This is the lowest temp every recorded here in the month of April in this area. So once again, please bundle up and make sure your elderly neighbors are okay during this time. Check your pilot lights for those who use gas heat. Now for our next story.

"Is the DMZ heating up again? After the second conflict between North Korea and South Korea, there seems to be more tension than the norm, and things seem to be heating up. Troop movement on the north side seems to have tripled on the northern side of the DMZ. The US is moving more troops to reinforce the troops already there.

"Tech units already deployed in the area have been ordered to stand at full alert status. Those who were coming home are still doing so, but their leave will be cut short and will return in two weeks.

"In related news, Congress has reenacted the draft, and all healthy males and females ages eighteen to thirty-five are to report for a full physical to determine if they are ready for combat training. The Russia Republic is posturing military parades to show it has regained its former strength and glory."

The news Jeff had just heard bothered him greatly because his wife was still coming home but would return back to duty even though she was planning on going in to the reserves and getting out of full-time service. However, now she would be unable to do so because of the alert and threat posed by North Korea.

10

This Can't Continue

JASON AND JANE made it in a little late.

The storm door slammed behind them as it closed. The iron ornate door was heavy; if you did not hold it before it closed, it would slam shut.

"Hey, you two, there are some bags on your beds. Don't open them until morning. I think you will like them," their dad said as they came in.

Both replied in unison, "Okay." They went to their rooms.

After Jane dropped her books off at her room, she decided to take a walk. She enjoyed walking in the woods behind her house; there was a special spot she liked to go; it overlooked a meadow of wild flowers.

The place was very quiet, no sound except nature. The stump she sat on when she would go there was like any other, except the flowers seemed to grow on the stump as if God had made that place just for her.

When she got there, she looked over the blooming wild flowers, knowing tonight's cold snap would kill them. Jane sat on the stump, and as always, the seat was dry, no moisture anywhere.

She looked over the field; it was very relaxing. She often talked to God about anything under the sun.

Today, she would do the same. "Lord, I come to you and beg you for forgiveness of my sins.

"Lord, please give me and my brother Jason the courage and strength to continue this battle before us. Lord, thank you for this day and the wonderful flowers that I see today.

"Lord, be with my mom and the troops as well. Thank you for all the blessing you have given me and my family.

"In your name. Amen."

When she did, the flowers in the field gave off a wonderful scent and it was easing her mind, and somehow she knew what she and her brother had to do, and that was to stick to the fight.

The next morning, both Jane and Jason opened the bags and saw T-shirts with the text which read on the front, "God or GPA—which is greater?"

On the back, it had a Bible verse. "Proverbs 3:5– 'With all your heart, trust in the Lord and not your own understanding.'"

Both Jason and Jane came down stairs wearing the brightly colored T-shirts, smiling from ear to ear.

"Thanks, Dad. This is great. I like the verse too. It's hard to beat a great proverb."

Jane agreed with Jason's comment on the shirts.

"Dad, could you make more? I think maybe this will get some attention at school."

"I can make as many as you two want. I have about thirty made up already."

"Great. We may be back with lots of orders."

"How much will they cost?"

"You know what, I'm going to eat the cost as long as it's school staff and students, and if any one else wants them, the price will be ten bucks. Only one shirt per student. Otherwise, they will have to pay for any extra they get."

Not many people had seen Jason's shirt until he walked into class.

"Mr. Harrper, let me see what that shirt says please," Mr. Parks said.

Jason stood up proudly to show it off.

"Hmmm, GPA or God… I see. Well, I think my answer would be GPA. Now go to the bathroom and turn that shirt inside out so no one can see it."

"Wait, Mr. Parks, you need to read the back."

"Mr. Harrper, go now and fix your shirt!"

"No," he said flatly.

"What did you say, young man?"

"I said, no, I will not cover up God's word."

"Young man, if you don't do as I ask, I will send you to the office."

"What you're asking is wrong, what you're asking me to do is the very thing I'm protesting for."

"You have gone too far, Mr. Harrper. It's time you went to the office."

"You're going to have to take me. I refuse to cover God's words," Jason said defiantly.

"Very well. Let's go then."

On the way to the office, chants could be heard from outside. "God is better than GPA!"

The shouts were getting louder as they got closer to the office. Jason heard the shouts, and he could not hold it in any longer.

"Mr. Parks, this is bigger than you and me. This has gotten everyone's attention now."

Mr. Parks stopped in the hall and looked out on one of the empty classroom windows and saw the picket signs. Parents and school staff were protesting the teaching of evolution and the big bang theory.

"Mr. Harrper, explain to me what is going on. Did you have anything to do with this?"

"No, sir, but I know who did." Jason smiled as he saw his dad out the window.

"Who is responsible for this?"

Jason just smiled. "Why, God is responsible for this. Not to mention the Christians in this town finally got up and decided to fight for God. That's all that is going on here."

They finally made it to the office, and at that point, Mr. Parks was so mad all he saw was red.

When they got to the office, it was full of parents who seemed very fired up about the issue because their kids took on a fight that God put before them when they did not and left it for their kids to fight it, so in order to make up for it or at least try to, they decided to help their kids with the fight now. Mr. Hall walked up to Mr. Parks. "I have to say one thing. You sure got this town fired up, Mr. Parks. They are demanding you resign your job here and move on. However, I'm not going to do that nor is the superintendent. We agree that your job is safe. Now what's this?"

"Mr. Harrper here has defied me and disturbed my class for the last time. I want him suspended for wearing obscene fashion. He refused to turn his shirt inside out when I asked him to. Read what it says."

"Hmm, I think you forget where you are and who I am."

"What do you mean, Mr. Hall?"

"We had this discussion before."

"I am a Christian first, a deacon of my church, then a principal of this school."

"Mr. Hall, don't fire him. We need him just as much as he needs us."

Mr. Hall smiled at what Jason had just said. "It seems, Mr. Parks, that our kids are smarter than we are. Why do you say that, Jason?"

"He needs to learn more about God, and we needed a reason to stand up for Christ, and he gave that to us. I mean look around you. Everyone here is fired up because of Mr. Parks."

"Don't you mean because of you and your sister?"

"No, sir, without you, there would be no fight, and without the fight, this town would still be stepping to the side and going around the battle God has put before them. You see, you gave us a reason to stand strong for God, and since we did not wish to put up with false teachings, we decided to fight for what we were taught even though others had stepped aside in this battle long ago. You see, we could not."

"I simply can't put faith in something I can't see. I have always trusted science and its cold, hard facts. I simply do not know what to think. However, it does not change the fact of what is being taught, and I must abide by that."

Outside, the local news crew and the local papers were outside finding out what was going on.

"We're here outside the local high school to find out what this demonstration is about. There are signs saying 'We will not stand for false teachings,' and others read, 'God is more important than GPA.' I have found the ring leader for this protest: Jeff Harrper. The reporter looking around, he saw some people wearing the T-shirts that Jason and Jane were wearing. So, Mr. Harrper, why now? Why this subject? Has it not already been decided by the courts over twenty years ago?"

"Yes, by man's law, it has, but our kids have decided differently, and being a member of the generation that stepped to the side to avoid the fight, I'm sad to say we as Christians stepped aside this issue, and now our children are having to fight this battle that we should have taken care of back then. You called me the ring leader. I cannot take that credit, for it was my kids who started this, and they intend on finishing it."

"Mr. Harrper, what if only your children are the only ones taking part in this protest?"

"Knowing them two, they will stick with it, leaving a message that we all should take responsibility for our actions and the battles God puts before us. We simply cannot pick and choose our fights that we know or think we can win."

"So even if you were to lose your business because you stand for God, you would still do so?"

Jeff looked the lady reporter in the eyes and with all seriousness gave his reply, "Yes. Money is of little use in heaven. The Lord will give me what I need, but I stand here guilty of stepping to the side back then, but my children did not. They answered the call that God sent to them as I and others should have done back then. I'm very proud of them."

Mr. Parks did not know what to make of the protest outside the school and how some of the parents got really into it.

It did not take long, however, for those who did not believe did come up to start a demonstration of their own with signs reading, "God Is a Fake" and others that read "Fools Follow Fairytales."

The shouts that were aimed at the Christians started to get downright offensive.

It did not take long for a fight to break out.

Mr. Parks dashed out of the office and ran to the front door of the school and out to the fight.

"STOP THIS! STOP THIS MADNESS NOW! This is not how Christians act. Now stop this!"

"How would you know how a Christian should act?" someone countered.

"Because two of my students are prime examples of how Christians should act. This is not it." He then turned around and marched back inside. He then told Jason to return to class.

Jason noticed something different about Mr. Parks when he came back in. He could not put his finger on it, but he knew something was going on.

By lunch time, every student had a T-shirt like Jason's and Jane's, which seemed to anger and confuse Mr. Parks even more.

He himself did not understand how this Jesus, who is long dead, could have this kind of effect on a normal person.

Around three o'clock, the crowd broke up and left to get their kids from school, thus ending the days protest.

After school, Mr. Parks became more curious why someone would stand up for a dead man.

So like anybody he decided to do some research, and the first thing to do was to buy a Bible and read it. He also did a little research online. Maybe he could figure this out and gain some understanding of why this was happening.

11

Why?

Mr. Parks read the entire book of Genesis. As he was doing it, he thought to himself he should know that book by heart; he had seen enough of it from his students to almost quote the whole thing, but he had read it anyway.

Reading the book seemed to make him think about both evolution and creation; both had their points, but both seemed so out in the left field, both theories should have been dismissed a long time ago.

He often wondered why Christians trusted in a God that no one could see; he remembered when he was a child his great-grandfather had told him, "If you be quiet and be real still, and listen, you just might hear God speak." He often said that when he wanted Tim to hush.

Tim smiled at the memories of his great-grandfather, and then he decided to find out why those two Harrper kids hold on to their faith so much with all that has been happening in defending their faith is that they were sacrificing their studies and hurting their chances of getting into a good college he knew they both deserved to be in.

So to figure out why they believe the way they, do he decided to read the entire Bible and do as much research as he could on the subject.

As he got further into it, the Bible started to make sense to him, and he also was learning on faith and why it was one of the cornerstones of Christianity and how love was another; however, he did find any kind of hateful passages. He only found lessons and laws and rules just as he had been told, what to do, what not to do, and how to live his life according to God.

Tim called his son into the living room with a new kind of understanding of how they believed. "Son, I'm not sure yet, but I think I might agree with them, and if so, I would like you to as well."

"But, Dad, in the Bible, it says what I'm doing is an abomination I'm going to hell according that."

"No, son, you're not. From what I have read, you're not."

"I'm not?"

"If you take Christ into your life, he will forgive you of all your sins. Not to mention you have never had feelings toward men, not to mention girls. You simply dress that way, so I would not worry."

12

The Test

Mr. Parks worked hard on this test; he had finally figured a few things out, and with some research, he had come up with a weekly test that he hoped all would take.

On Monday morning, Mr. Parks did not walk into his class with dread; he seemed a bit happy.

"Class, we are still on the same subject I have been teaching. However, instead of using just our textbooks, we will also use this one." He then held up the Bible and started passing out the King James Version to everyone.

"I am going to make a personal statement first, so then you may understand why I am choosing to do this.

"First off, some things came to me when that fight broke out Friday, and then what I said to stop it made me think. So I bought this Bible to find out why Christians would do this fight for a dead man.

"I read this Word of God and found it made a lot of good points, and then I discovered you are not fighting for a dead man. You are fighting for a living Son of God as well as God himself.

"So since you have written about your version of the creation of man and the world, each question and the subject matter will deal with what we have covered in class and what the Bible says on the subject. Each question will have two answers, one from the text book and one from the Bible. Then you will mark which one you truly believe. I'm not to where I can say I trust Christ; however, I am not done researching this either. I may go to a church this Sunday just to see what it's about."

Jason walked up to Mr. Parks after class.

"Mr. Parks, would you like to go to the revival.

"Jason, what is a revival?"

"Well, Mr. Parks, it's a preaching and rekindling in your heart of the sprit of Jesus Christ. It starts tonight, and I would meet you there. You would have a friend there so no one will bother you, and you can search yourself and find out what is going on in your heart."

"Mr. Harrper, I think I might just do that. Could I meet you at your house though?"

"Sure, no problem. If you come around five, you can eat with us, and maybe Dad can talk to you about how you're feeling."

"I would like that. Five it is, then."

After school, Jason and Jane ran home to get ready for church. They were both excited about Mr. Parks and Seth coming to dinner, so was Jeff, who was very willing to explain who Christ is.

Mr. Parks arrived at five as he said, and he brought Seth as well, which gave Jason and Jane a chance to talk about salvation to him and let him know he was not a lost cause in God's eyes.

They knew that telling him he was going to burn if he did not trust Christ was the wrong approach and was always the wrong one fire and brimstone and wrath was wrong because someone searching for the Lord needed to know of his love and mercy.

They knew they had to show God's mercy and his love for all his creations, not just a chosen few.

Jeff welcomed them into his home, and as they were coming in, the smell of freshly grilled steaks filled the air.

"Hello, Mr. Parks. This must be your son, Seth, if I'm not mistaken." Jeff extended his hand, and Mr. Parks shook his hand with friendship. "Jason and Jane are up stairs in the game room. Why don't you go up there, and you can do whatever until supper is ready, which won't be long."

Jason was coming down the stairs when he saw Seth going up.

"Hey, come on up. I was just coming to see who was at the door. We got a good game of bumper pool going on, and Jane is losing for once."

They both laughed, and then Jason noticed what Seth was wearing.

"Hey, I thought you normally wear more girlish clothes?"

"I do, but I did not want to offend anyone by my clothes, so I wore this suit."

"It looks good on you."

"Thanks. I feel a little strange in it though."

"You will be fine. Don't worry."

"Jason, Seth can take your sister's place. She needs to set the table. Would you please tell her?" Jeff called out.

"So, Mr. Parks—"

"Tim, please. I thank you for the invitation for dinner and the revival. I have a lot of questions and few answers. Maybe you can help me with some of them."

"I would be glad to help. I will do my best to help you."

"First thing is my son. The Bible says what he is doing is an abomination. Is my son headed to hell for doing what he has been doing?"

"No, of course not. First off, according to Jason, he has had no interest in guys or girls, so what he is doing is not an abomination. He is simply confused about who he is. Not to mention, Christ forgives all. You see, once you ask Jesus into your heart, the Lord washes your sin away with the blood he spilled when he was crucified on the cross. God knows we are going to sin. So he sent his son to die on the cross, and through his son, our sins are cleansed, thus we can get into heaven.

"So Jesus will forgive even murder?"

"Yes, he does. He even will forgive you of lying in bed with another member of the same gender. It's not unforgivable. Now don't get me wrong. Being a Christian is not easy, for you have to forsake a lot of things you might have enjoyed doing. However, we are only human and are going to mess up a lot.

"No sin is greater than another. To God, sin is sin, and he hates all sin, but he does not hate the sinner. That is the most important thing you must understand. God hates sin, not the person who commits the sin. In the Bible, it states the wages of sin is death, but then it says, 'Whosoever believes in me shall have everlasting life.' Which is it? Both. You see, we are born into a world of sin and are already dead, but through Jesus, we are reborn as children of God."

"I see, I think I understand. I even think I understand why you defend a dead man. That's because he is not dead. He is alive I think I get it now. Though I am still unsure about a lot of things."

"If you want, I will try to help you understand those things so you can become closer to God."

Both Tim and Seth had a lot to think about. One could tell that God was dealing with them both.

After dinner, they went to the revival. It was at the park under a huge tent because of the impending cold weather coming.

The sermon was on faith, and in fact, it seemed as if the entire message was meant for Mr. Parks and his son.

The sky was lit brightly by a full moon and the twinkling of stars in the night sky. The air was a bit crisp, but jackets kept them comfortable. The weather had been a bit on the odd side there as of late, with snow and ice in the middle of April.

After the service, Tim started talking to the preacher and asking him questions on things he did not understand.

"Brother Jack, how is it you're so sure that Christ is truly the son of God, and what makes you think God even exists?"

"Walk with me. Your son is welcome to join. I will show you truth, and as for facts, there is abundance of proof that God is the creator."

Tim kept looking around, but no one seemed angered by his presence. Some even looked happy and walked over and shook his hand, saying, "Welcome."

"A few days ago, they were ready to hang me on the flag pole. Now they are welcoming me. I'm confused."

"When you came outside and said that is not how Christians should act and when someone asked you how would you know, you pointed out two prime examples. You see, you made them think. Once they thought about it, they knew you had seen true Christian action. They knew the way they were acting was wrong and decided to make it right since they had the opportunity to do that tonight. Now let me show you proof God is real."

They walked up to a huge very old oak tree. It stood nearly a hundred feet tall, and it had huge branches going all the way up.

"You see the tree right here?" Brother Jack patted the huge tree.

"Yes, I do."

"First, a fact: everything on earth points up, does it not?"

"Yes, of course."

"Flowers point to the sun for nourishment when the sun shines, and they still do it when it rains. Some flowers fold their petals when the moon comes out, and some fold when they are cold to protect themselves from the cold. You see this old tree here, no matter how harsh life has treated it, still stands and shows its beauty to all."

"Now we as Christians should do the same to glorify our Lord and Savior. However we sometimes forget God and only thank Jesus for everything."

"Nature glorifies God by doing what they are supposed to do, which is provide air as God intended on it to do. Some plants also provide medicines for us to keep us healthy and make us feel better."

"I'm surprised you know so much about science."

"Why is that?"

"You see, I guess you being a man of God you are all about God, but there is more to you than that."

"Oh, I see. Well, I am all about God. However man forgot what science is truly about."

"And what is that?"

"Science is about discovery and knowledge on how things on this world works and how it can benefit us.

However, science forgot its true meaning, and now it has been corrupted by man to make weapons and chemicals that are destroying the earth God has made. These weather conditions are our own doing throughout the years of not caring.

"Science in its flurry to understand how everything was made came up with one of the most ridiculous theories anyone has heard, yet it has been accepted as fact because people are in such a hurry to believe in anything except God. So here is a question: how was the earth made?"

"The big bang."

"Well, if the big bang occurred, what caused it?"

"Some gases combined and caused a great explosion, creating the planet."

"So where did the gases come from?"

"Cosmic dust combined in such a way that various gases came to be."

"Where did that come from?

"Science has not got that far yet."

"Science may not have gone that far, but God has. You see, the science Christian argument ends with God winning every round. Now for man."

"I get your point. Science is circular in thinking when it comes to origin."

"If all this happened by accident, how did a complicated ecosystem come to be? How did the animals and all of God's beings develop complicated systems on their own?

All of this was planned out, carefully designed by God. Now with that in your mind, I want you to remember some history. We will start with World War II.

"Hitler was so evil he hated everything about the Jews, God's chosen people, so he set out to destroy them. When Hitler's armies marched across Europe, he was unstoppable until for some strange reason, things started to go wrong. What happened was God kept Hitler asleep during the D-day invasion, thus keeping a large number of forces sitting on their rears waiting for orders. In turn they had to stay there, and we won the war from there on in."

"Well, I could argue that he took a sleeping pill."

"Yes, but what made him take it at such an important time of the war, knowing an attack was coming?"

"I don't know. I was not him."

"So history is full of God's divine intervention, and even today, you can see it unfold. I'm going to ask you to do something. I want you to read the Bible from a historical point of view. Do as much research as you need to. Then come back and talk to me. I will be here for the next two weeks. Come back and listen and, if possible, learn something about God and Jesus. I am going to be a little bit bold here, Tim. I think that the Lord is already dealing with you, and you are already deciding on which way to make your decision. Now this is where free will comes into play. This is a choice you must make on your own. We can only give you advice and all the truths you need to know, but in the end, it's your choice. Simply put, your relationship to God is just between you and Almighty God as well as his son Jesus Christ."

Tim looked at his watch. "It's getting late. Maybe we could get together this weekend for lunch or dinner and talk about this more."

"I would like that very much, Tim."

Jeff had walked and had heard the tale end of the talk between Tim and the preacher. "I have an idea. Why don't we grill out at my house on Saturday around twelve noon."

They all agreed that would be the perfect place to continue the discussion.

13

Mom's Home!

AFTER THE REVIVAL, they all went their separate ways. When Jeff and the kids got home, they noticed that the lights were on. They knew they turned them off before they left.

"Is someone in our house?"

"Let me check and make sure it's safe."

Jeff got out of the car, and as he did, Stacy walked outside dressed in her army uniform.

When Jane and Jason saw their mom, they jumped out of the car excitedly.

"Mom, Mom!"

"You're home!"

"Sorry, guys, but it's not for long. I got to be back in two weeks."

"I heard. Is it really getting that bad?"

"Yes, it is, Jeff. It's very bad."

"Before I left, the North had gotten about twenty miles into the South when a South Korean unit shot at them, running them back across the border."

"My CO thinks the very reason they were there was to see how tight our security is. But let's not talk about that. I wish to spend time with you and the kids."

Despite the fact that Stacy was home, the kids had to go to bed, so they could go to school in the morning.

The next morning, Jason and Jane woke up to the smell of their favorite blueberry pancakes. They came running downstairs to see who was cooking, and of course, it was Stacy getting the meal ready while Jeff was getting ready for work.

Just as always, Jeff sat down in front of the TV to catch the news.

"Good morning, everyone, and welcome to Channel 12 News."

"First up, the weather."

"Chad, what do you have for us?"

"Today we have highs of ninety-eight degrees, and today's lows is eighty-seven degrees. It's also going to be very hot the rest of the week, including the weekend. It will be a scorcher. Temperatures are going to reach the three-digit mark and stay that way until Wednesday on our future cast, and we are also tracking a very cold front Thursday and Friday. Back to you, Sally."

"Now for the national news."

"In Washington, DC, Congress passed a resolution that states that any nonprofit organization has to pay taxes for the past five years. The IRS has issued a warning to all such groups and are expected to pay with in the next three months. According to economic analysts, this will help pay at least two-thirds of the national debt."

Jeff turned off the TV and went into the kitchen to give Stacy a good-bye kiss.

"Jeff, I will bring lunch by since I have the time for now."

"Hmm, how about I take you to lunch. After all, I know the boss very well."

Stacy smiled.

"So do I."

Then they kissed.

Jason and Jane watched them give each other a kiss, and both of them started making kissing noises.

"Cool it, you two."

"Aw, we were just having a little fun."

"Yes, now that breakfast is over. You two can have fun at school."

Jane and Jason both laughed and started making the noise again as they ran out the door.

14

Enforced

THE REST OF the day was uneventful. Mr. Parks seemed occupied with thoughts about the existence of God, and it was having an impact on how he was teaching the subject at hand.

"Brother Macey, this came in the mail. It's from the IRS. They are going to want taxes for the past five years and are sending someone down to go through our books to find out how much we owe," Bill, the treasurer of the First Baptist Church of Texas, reported.

"Well, we have to abide what the word says. 'Give Cesar what is his and give God what is his,' which is the Lord comes first as always. But, sir, but we cant afford taxes for the past five years."

Bill was very worried about the letter he had received informing them if they did not comply with the agent, all the church properties would be seized and sold at auction to the highest bidder.

"Brother Macey, they are to be here on Wednesday around four, just an hour before church services start. What are we going to do?"

"I'm sure they will be understanding and wait for business to be done on Thursday. Don't worry so much, Bill. God shall protect us. We have nothing to hide, and as big as we are, I'm sure the amount we owe is nothing we can't handle, even if we have to mortgage some of our properties to pay it. We may have to struggle a bit, but I'm sure our members will pitch in and help us."

"I'm glad you have a cool head like that. As for me, I'm worried."

"Bill, you need to worry more about that pizza sauce on your shirt. I have faith in the Almighty. He has shown me things that prove to me he is with us. We may not like his answers at times, but it will all go according to his will."

"Such as?"

"Those kids in that news story where they stood up against the teachings of evolution and the big bang stood up, and from what I have heard, the teacher is teaching both sides of the fence so as not to anger the government."

"How do you know this?"

"The pastor there is a friend of mine."

"Also, the teacher as well as his son are starting to change his mind about God."

"So, Brother Macey, do we go ahead with Wednesday's service as planned?"

"Yes, I think that will be okay if we do so. It's not like we are a bunch of armed thugs hoarding guns and stuff to take life."

Agent Will Easton was assigned to look at the books of the First Baptist Church of Texas.

He did not take kindly to delays, even if it meant disrupting business as usual, even if it was a church.

Agent Easton walked into the church around 5:15. He was running a little late. Church services had already started, and Agent Easton did not wish to wait. He entered the front door and saw everyone in prayer, but he did not care.

He announced himself as loud as he could to get everyone's attention. "I am Agent Will Easton from the IRS. You must cease what you're doing now!"

The entire congregation looked at the rather tall, thin man with balding spot right up front. Brother Macey asked agent Easton to wait.

"Mr. Easton, please wait until the morning. You are bound to be tired. We can put you up in one of the mission homes we use to help those who have had a fire and need a place to stay. They are very nice."

"I will not wait, Pastor, and if you do not cease what you're doing, I will have twenty agents down here in five seconds!"

"What harm are we causing by praying to the Lord? Brother Phil, would you please take Mr. Easton here and show him the books, so he can get started if he wishes. Mr. Easton, I will answer your questions after service I am doing the Lord's work, and not even the mighty government will stop me."

"That is unacceptable. Everyone must leave now!"

No one got up. No one even raised their bowed heads. They kept praying.

"Mr. Easton, it would be better if we did this in the morning instead of interrupting the Lord's work tonight."

Agent Easton pulled his gun and called in an assault team. A few state troopers and one or two Texas Rangers were inside worshiping as well. When the assault team came in and opened fire, they drew their weapons to defend the people there.

The gun fire was deafening inside the huge church as young and old were shot down in cold blood. A smoke grenade was tossed into the church, and it filled with smoke, but it was too late. Most were injured from gunshots, and others had died.

One of the Texas Rangers had made it out and had called for help. "This is Ranger Jacks. The First Baptist Church of Texas is under attack. Almost every one is dead."

A call for all local and state units went out over the police band, and within seconds, over twenty rangers and local cops were surrounding the church.

Before anyone could identify themselves, someone from the IRS assault team opened fire, and the Rangers returned fire, killing Agent Easton and his entire team.

It was not long before the press heard about the incident, and the head of the Texas Rangers as well as the IRS had shown up at the scene within an hour during the investigation.

"This is Ann Landers of WKNA News reporting live from the First Baptist Church of Texas, which is now a bloody scene of carnage being attacked from unknown forces for a unknown reasons. No one knows as of yet why a heavily armed assault team would attack a church.

"Captain Stringer, I know who these people are, sir."

"Who are they, Sergeant Jacks?"

"Sir, he claimed he was from the IRS and demanded we stop service, then his team opened fire, killing a lot of the congregation including children."

"Captain, why would an IRS agent need a tactical team at a church?"

"Jacks, exactly what happened?"

"Like I said, he came in, and he identified himself as Agent Easton of the IRS. Then he pulled his weapon, called in his team, and they came in shooting."

"Where is the pastor?"

"Dead, sir."

All of what was being said was said loud enough for the reporters to hear, which was Captain Stringer's intention.

"This is Ann Landers coming to you with a breaking news here at the First Baptist Church of Texas with an update. We have just learned who the assault team was. It was the IRS. And leading them was Agent Will Easton, who he himself was killed in the fire fight. Among the dead were two four-year-old twins shot and killed as well as their eighty-nine-year-old great-grandmother.

"Some of the survivors state that they opened fire without provocation. All they did was sit and pray when the IRS busted in and interrupted the church service, and in a time of prayer no less.

"More words on casualties, the pastor of the church as well as the entire choir were shot and killed. This is my personal opinion, but I think this was a big misuse of power by the IRS. And questions are being asked why would an agent of the IRS need a tactical assault team to enter a church.

"Just arriving on the scene is the director of the IRS, Pete Sanders. Mr. Sanders, can you tell us why an assault team was needed to enter a church here? Can you answer why

Agent Easton even came to the church during the evening worship service instead of the morning when nothing would be going on except day-to-day business instead of a time when the church is having service?"

"No comment! I said, no comment!"

"This is Ann Landers, interviewing one of the survivors. What is your name, miss?"

"My name is Kim Thaxton."

"So by your account, what really happened in there?"

Kim started tearing up a bit as she tried to answer the question.

"The agent identified himself, and some of the law enforcement that go to our church stood up to defend us when the agent and his team opened fire. That's when the rangers and state troopers returned fire. Those people... why did they have to kill my friends and family?"

"For way too long, people have been siding with the government on issues of church and state, and this is a real issue of church and state."

"Those brutes killed my family and friends."

Kim could no longer keep it together as she finally fell into uncontrollable sobbing.

"You have heard it hear first, an actual account of what happened inside the church. The IRS gunned down these people in the church without provocation. This all has happened in a country where freedom of religion is one of the cornerstones of the constitution.

"Also some law enforcement officers were shot and killed. Among those that survived were Texas Ranger Sergeant Andrew Jacks and Texas State Trooper Ray Mullins, who also gave the same accounts as the rest of the survivors.

"This is Ann Landers reporting to you live from the First Baptist Church of Texas. We will bring you all the updates as we get them."

Jeff was angered and disgusted from what he had just seen on the news.

The news broke in again with a new update.

"This is Ann Landers with a news update on those wounded during tonight's shooting at the First Baptist Church of Texas. We have learned that the lieutenant governor was injured severely and is now recovering at the hospital."

15

Hiding the Truth

At the IRS building the next morning.

A GENT READER SAID, "Sir, it's all over the news. How are we going to cover this up? The lieutenant governor was at the church when Agent Easton's team shot up the place. Not to mention that Reporter Ann Landers has this story sweeping the nation, and even some international news agencies have gotten a hold of the story."

"It has spread like a fire storm overnight," Agent Reader continued.

"That is the bad thing about the reporters. They get it out before you can do anything about it," Director Sanders said.

"We start with the highest official there and see if we can get him to discredit the story. Then we go from there."

"Sir, I think this is going to fail miserably."

"Oh, and, sir, don't ask me to do this because, sir, I will quit."

"Agent Reader, you will do as I say!"

Agent Reader, without saying a word, laid his badge, weapon, and a letter of resignation on the desk and walked out of the office.

"Director Sanders, the president is on the phone, and he does not sound happy."

President Clark was very angry about the whole situation and wanted answers.

"Mr. Sanders, how the hell did something like this happen. Why would he need a tactical team to go over the books at a church? It's bad enough you guys have such a bad rap as it is, but now your agency is responsible for over fifty deaths and over a hundred injured, and more still can die from their wounds! I WANT ANSWERS, AND I WANT THEM NOW!

"One other thing, you and your agency will be completely open about this. No cover-up. Don't try to get to anyone so you can discredit the story. You will give a statement, and we will pay compensation to those who died and all those who were in the church. IF I EVEN HAVE AN IDEA OF A COVER-UP, I WILL PUT YOU IN PRISON FOR A VERY LONG TIME!"

Mr. Sanders's face was blood-red from the chewing out he was getting from the commander in chief himself, and the fact he said *prison* had put the fear of God in him so to speak.

President Clark slammed the phone down, leaving Mr. Sanders sitting in shock and wondering what he was going to do.

The next day, Ann Landers had gotten more information about the shooting and a good side story from the people at the church who had gone to clean up the mess and fix the church back up to its original state.

"Good morning, Texas. This is Ann Landers with more updates on last night's shooting at the First Baptist Church of Texas.

"As you know, an IRS agent named Will Easton took a tactical assault team with him to determine how much the church would owe in taxes. He went in disturbing our God-given right to worship."

"We have a video footage of what happened from a camera that was recording the service as they always have done so they can post their service on the web so those that can't go can also enjoy the service at home.

"You can see here Agent Easton making his demands as he give no notice of a armed response from him he simply picked up his radio and called an armed tactical team into the church of worshippers and was no threat to anyone."

"The first to die was the pastor and the entire choir, including the organist and piano player. Most of the first through the fifth rows of pews received most of the gun fire. It did not matter how old or young they were. It did not matter to them."

Still on air, the reporter had to pause a moment to dry her tears and try to regain herself and continue with the story.

"The heads of the church, as well as its members, have stated that their constitutional rights have been violated and plan on filing a lawsuit against the IRS for preventing them from worshiping God."

"In related news, the governor has called an emergency meeting to discuss plans as to what to do and see about pressing criminal charges against the IRS. Also, Governor Richards has ordered the national guard to the IRS building to protect the people who work there."

Inside the State Congress Hall.

"Ladies and Gentlemen, we have a very serious issue here, and it needs to be dealt with swiftly. Does anyone have any suggestions as to how to go about this?"

One of the senate members, Barbie Anderson, stood to speak. "If you ask me, I think this a clear violation of Texas law, and I think we should secede from the union and become the Republic of Texas once again."

Governor Richards rubbed his beard in thought.

"I believe my research is right, sir, when we joined the union, if the United States violated Texas law to such a degree, we have the right to secede from the union at will."

"Senator Anderson, I think you may have something there. We must look deeper into this fact, and if the United States has indeed violated Texas law so bad, I then think we should secede from the union."

After some discussion, for once, every member of the Senate and Congress had agreed on what to do next.

16

Where Does Shame Come From?

TIM HAD BEEN thinking a lot about how much he needed something new in his life, something filling; and after the revival, he seemed to need more time to think things through.

The biggest question on his mind was, is God real? He had been doing a scientific study as well as historical study to find out where the concept of where God came from.

Both studies proved one thing, and that was science indeed had a more circular line of thinking; it did not seem to have a straight line. As the version the Bible, it had a beginning and an eventual end.

As it was said in Revelation 22:13 (KJV), "I am the alpha and the omega the beginning and the end."

He decided he needed a peaceful place to think, so he went to go to the court square and sit and think for a while.

He now had the questions and some of the answers, but where should he put them to which question?

Tim saw no one in the little park, so he walked around and read quote on the old statue again, and all he could make out was, "Through faith, all things are possible."

A hand touched Tim's shoulder, nearly scaring him out of his shoes.

"Hiya, Tim, how's it going, my friend? I hear the Lord is dealing with you and your son."

Tim looked up and saw Zeak, the old black man who had served his country long ago. He still carried his Bible in the old courier bag.

Tim smiled and extended his hand and shook hands.

"I'm okay, I guess, and I think you may be right about God dealing with me and my son, but I still can't answer the question you asked me."

"And what question was that?"

"Where did shame come from?"

"So did you come up with at least an idea as to where it came from?"

"Well, I have a thought. Shame started in the garden of Eden. When God had seen that both had sinned against him, they felt shame. I know that much but I'm not sure of where it came from." Tim then had a thought. "What if shame was in us to start with? What if that emotion came when they knew they had done wrong? What if it was a punishment to both of them?"

"You're starting to catch on, Tim, but to me shame is when man sinned against God, they felt shame for the first time. Shame was felt. Embarrassment was felt. For they were naked before God. Adam and Eve had made garments from fig leaves to cover themselves, for they knew they were naked. However does shame come from man, or does it come from God?

"You know, Tim, I think everyone simply needs to accept shame is a result of sin. Where does it come from, God or the devil?"

"I'm not sure, but it's a question that makes one think, doesn't it?"

"Tim, you're starting to figure things out. You're thinking about sin, and sin is of the devil."

"Why do I believe your catching on Tim?"

"There is so much that I don't understand. How can I serve him if I don't know much?"

"That's easy, Tim. The best you can. You see, God left a book, the very one you called a fairytale. That is how you learn from his word."

"What about all the revisions of the Bible? It has been rewritten so many times."

"Yes, but its core purpose stays the same: to guide you through life. Whatever is left out overtime, we learn through our own lives—if we listen to the Lord, that is."

"I have so many questions to ask."

"Look, I'm an old man, and I don't have but maybe an ounce of understanding as to what the Lord wants from me. I can't tell you the whole story. No one can, but my favorite saying is, 'Through faith, all things are possible.' You see, everything is based on faith. Even science is based on it, if you look at it. The Lord said if you have the faith the size of a mustard seed, you could move mountains."

"What do I do now?"

"That I can tell you. It's simple really, and you yourself know that answer. Since you look confused, I will tell you. You need to accept Jesus into your heart as your Lord and Savior. That's what you need to do."

Tim sat there on the bench next to Zeak, but when he turned to talk to him, Zeak's head was off on his shoulder like he was asleep. Zeak had collapsed.

"Zeak. Zeak, are you okay? Zeak!" Tim got his cell phone and called for help. He took his pulse, but he could not find one; he knew he was gone. He had passed on and not died, for he had the Lord deep in his heart.

At the hospital, a nurse came up to Tim. "Mr. Parks, we found this in Zeak's bag. It's a letter to you."

> Tim, please forgive me if my writing is a bit hard to read, so here is the thing: I have known for some time the Lord will call me home soon.
>
> Don't fret though. I am with God the Father, and I am singing with them angels. I always loved singing in church.

Now since you're reading this here letter, I've gone home to see the Lord.

I was worried about something though. I don't want you making a profession of faith because of me. I want you to do it because of you. Do it for the one person who counts in this case: you. Do it for you, and your son will follow, I'm sure of it.

Well, I think all God needed me to do is done, and I hope I helped out some.

If I passed when I finished talking to you, then my job is truly done here on earth.

God bless you, Tim Parks, and your son as well.

Zeak

Tearfully, Tim folded the letter gently and put it in his shirt pocket. He knew what he had to do, and it was now up to him to make the choice. Tim made the only true choice anyone could make.

Tim walked to the chapel in the hospital, then got down on his knees and asked the Lord into his heart.

"Lord, I have always said you were a fairytale, and now I believe otherwise. Please forgive me of my sins and let me into your light. Please, oh Lord, help me guide my son to you so he to can be saved. Amen."

A pastor who was standing to the side of the chapel when Tim came in had heard every word and walked up to Tim.

"My son, I saw you come in and was going to speak to you first, but I see you had someone else you needed to speak to, so I waited. I am glad for you that you have found the way in the light of the Lord. If there is anything I can do, simply come back by here."

"I will and thank you."

Tim then walked out of the chapel and went home to talk with his son.

17

Will You Defend Us?

THE PHONE RANG at the Harrper household.

Jeff picked it up as he was about to leave to go to work. "Hello?"

"May I speak to Stacy please?"

"Who is calling?"

"I'm General Nathan Kimbel of the First Texas Army Division."

"Hang on a minute. She will be right here." Then he called out, "Stacy! Phone!"

Stacy came and took the phone. "Hello?"

"Is this Major Stacy Harrper?"

"Yes, what can I do for you, General?"

"By order of the governor, we have left the union. I have been put in charge of the First Texas Army, and I need to know if you're on board with us, or will you be sticking with the US Military."

"After what I saw on the news, I will be honored to be a part of the First Texas Army."

"Then congratulations is in order. You are now a colonel. You should come down here so we can make it official."

"Where is that?"

"Same place we always meet. All men and women of the armed forces stationed here in Texas will be given the choice, and we plan on respecting their choice as to whom they serve."

"I have heard nothing about this on the news yet."

"You won't. Not yet. The US government does not know, but I do think they suspect. As of now, none of this is truly official yet. It all depends on what happens with the investigation of why this happened and what they intend on doing about it."

"I understand, sir."

"I will brief you more on what is going on so you will be more informed."

"I'm on my way, sir."

Stacy hung up the phone and told Jeff what she was told and then left with a need for Jeff to pray for his wife and all those that were concerned.

Jeff was on his way to work when a breaking news update come on.

"This is Ann Landers with breaking news! California is experiencing a massive earthquake that has lasted for the past thirty minutes and has not ceased. Some geologists say in their the state will sink into the ocean if the quakes do not stop soon. We will have updates as we get them. This is Ann Landers."

The music came back on. A shocked Jeff had to pull over to catch his breath. He then got out of his car, got on his knees, and prayed for all those in California.

He was compelled to do this as he knew time was getting close, and he knew it.

Jeff now had a lot more to worry about. Things seemed to be happening very quickly. More of the Bible was being fulfilled left and right these days.

The day had went into noon, and since it was lunchtime, Mr. Parks decided to talk to Jason and Jane about the decision he had just made about giving his life over to Christ.

The lunchroom was crowded as usual. Jason and Jane sat together and were having lunch with their friends.

"Hi, Jason, Jane, may I sit with you? I need to talk to you. It's really important."

"Uh, Jason, if Mr. Parks needs to talk to you, we can go find another table to eat at."

"No, please don't go. You may have something I might wish to hear about the subject."

Jason and Jane's friends had a look of shock on their faces; then they sat back down to hear what he had to say.

Seth then walked up, and he too was invited to sit with them.

Mr. Parks began, "I have found Christ, and I have made a decision to follow him, and I was hoping you could help me find my way."

"It seems to me you are finding your way already, Mr. Parks. All you need to do is trust him, learn as much as you can so you may serve him better."

"Thank you, Jason. However, I do still need help in understanding what I'm feeling."

Judy spoke up. "Mr. Parks, if you have doubts or questions, we all would be glad to help you out. Don't be afraid to ask even if it sounds stupid. We all need help, and we would be happy to help you get to know Christ."

"What about me?" Seth asked.

"Seth, that includes you as well."

"Thanks, guys.

"No problem."

Mr. Parks stayed and ate lunch with them and asked a few questions, and they all tried to answer his questions; however, if they did not have all the answers, they told him to look it up in the Bible or talk to a preacher.

At the Mississippi IRS Office.

Head of the Mississippi Division of the IRS.

Director Luke Simmons called in a lead agent to check out the churches in Mississippi.

"Sir, you wanted to see me?"

"Yes, Andy. You're going to have to take a tactical team with you after the uproar of what happened in Texas."

"I understand, sir. What church will we be auditing first?"

"It's a small Catholic church in Ecru, Mississippi called Saint Mary's. Also a second Baptist church in Thaxton. That is why I'm also assigning a second agent to go to that church. However, you will be in complete charge of both operations. Also there will be a second team to go with Agent Murry Atkins as well."

At the same time, the Texas IRS were making similar plans about two other churches in the area of Austin and Dallas.

Andy Faulks approached the church during a Wednesday night service. Andy busted in with the tactical team right behind him. "Cease what you are doing. I am Andy Faulks of the IRS."

Brother Thomas left the podium and approached Agent Faulks. Before Brother Thomas could get halfway to him, one of the members of the tactical team opened fire, and then an eruption of gun fire filled the church, killing everyone but two children, one of them being an infant who was protected by an eight-year-old boy named David Jones.

He stayed hidden, afraid to move for fear of being shot. He stayed hidden and kept the baby as quiet as possible.

"Oh crap, what happened? Who fired the shot?" Agent Faulks was really bewildered and terrified.

At Thaxton Baptist Church.

Agent Murry had walked in to the church, interrupting prayer service, using the same announcement as Agent Faulks had used.

Agent Murry saw Brother Malcome come down to meet him, but he was so afraid he pulled his gun, and he and his entire team killed everyone. No one was left alive.

After the smoke had cleared, Agent Murry sat down on the altar and uttered, "Not again."

Not knowing the same thing had happened at the other church.

The Dallas Church of Christ was assigned to Agent Wells and a team as well. Once again, the pastor stepped down to greet him, but instead of receiving some sort of greeting, a member of the team opened fire, and he fell to the ground covered in blood and lifeless. The congregation panicked.

It was less than an instant. The entire team opened fire, spraying the entire church with bullets. However, being fearful of the event happening like it did at the First Baptist Church of Texas.

So once again, law enforcement was there as well as the other churches instead of a slaughter of the churchgoers. Local police as well as one or two state troopers were present and returned fire as to defend those who were there. One of the officers called for help when they first arrived.

All the officers in the church who had been worshiping as well died during the firefight except for those waiting outside, and they were waiting with police assault vehicles, and the entire team and agents surrendered to them.

In Ecru and Thaxton, sirens sounded off in the distance.

About four sheriff cars arrived with an ambulance following close behind.

The same scene was taking place in Thaxton.

18

Under Fire

IT WAS THE morning after all the events, and everyone knew there was no way to contain this no matter how hard they tried, so the IRS did not even try.

The state of Mississippi was holding an emergency meeting to decide as what to do since the unthinkable had happened.

The state congress had agreed that something must be done for one of the countries main rights had been violated to the extreme. Governor John Andy Howard went before the state congress to give his thoughts on this situation.

"Ladies and gentlemen of congress, I come to you first as a citizen of Mississippi. Who am I kidding? Enough with speeches and political posturing. I come to you as a worried American and even more an afraid Christian!

"We must do something to protect our rights. We must consider the same thing that Texas is considering, and that is secede from the union and join Texas in doing this, thus creating our own country."

"Maybe they will get the idea. We as Americans will not tolerate these actions against any religion, and our religious rights have been violated time and time again. NOW IS THE TIME TO STAND UP AND FIGHT!"

The entire Congress was fired up, and all had stood up and applauded the governor.

Once they had calmed down enough to pay attention, he continued. "We have a duty to not just ourselves but to everyone in this state. We must think with clear heads and not act foolishly. We must make well-informed choices in deciding as what to do and how to do it.

"All ideas put before this assembly will be given consideration and voted on. For now, we must put the people of Mississippi first. We will not worry about our political careers. We must worry about the people."

Once again they applauded.

"Even though I myself am a Christian, we must think of the other religions as well, for they too will eventually fall victim to the same thing as we Christians have heard as of late.

"A very heinous crime has been committed by the IRS. I propose we look into all options as to what to do about this, including leaving the union and becoming our own nation.

"I have been discussing with the president of Texas about creating a new government that will honor the right to worship as we all see fit and to whom we worship as well.

"We need to return to a time of true values and not this politically correct garbage we all have had to endure from groups that have been called immoral from the beginning of time.

"In our new country, there will be the same rights as anyone else, and you can speak your mind without fear of someone trying to make your life miserable.

"We as a people have always seen things as moral and immoral, and we have not tolerated such behavior and have tried to end it. However this does not mean to go and try to ruin those who do these things.

"We know from what we have learned, no matter what religion we are, to hate the sin and not the sinner, just as those students in a small town in Texas did for that teacher and his son. They did not shun him or treat him badly. They spoke to him not just through words but through actions and kindness, and in the end he and his son both found God, and this is a prime example as how we should treat those who do not believe as well as those who simply don't wish to hear it."

As he finished speaking a thunderous applause erupted throughout the halls as everyone was in complete agreement.

The governor dismissed congress at the sound of the gavel.

As everyone was leaving and talking among themselves, most of the ideas were bad ones; however, one idea seemed to dominate everyone's thoughts form the union.

In Pontotoc, Mississippi.

West Heights Baptist Church was holding service at the time of the shooting when the all units were called both for fire and police. The radio could be heard as to what had happened, and Brother David dismissed the service with a short prayer.

"Lord, please be with those who have fallen worshiping you. Amen."

Then the entire congregation run to their cars and went to both churches.

The same thing was happening all over town. Churches were going out to help their brothers and sisters in Christ.

Those who arrived at St. Mary's Catholic Church found a very disturbing and very sad scene.

James, a deacon of West Heights Baptist Church, saw a young boy holding a baby. The boy looked very confused and lost. James walked over to the boy and kneeled down to speak to him.

"Hi, I'm James. Do you want me to hold the baby so you can rest? What's your name, little man?"

"I'm David Jones, sir."

"Do you know who this baby is?"

"Ms. Chrissy's baby. She lives next to me. She is dead now."

"Does Ms. Chrissy have a husband?"

David started to cry. It finally hit him that his mom and dad were both dead inside the church.

James found out he had an aunt in Tupelo, Mississippi. He got the number from David, who had it in his cowboy wallet he had gotten from her for Christmas this past year. They could not find a relative close by, so they would have to look for someone who could take care of the infant until someone could trace the family.

James took David to his home.

However, James knew there was nothing he could do to truly keep his mind off the fact he had lost the two most important people in his life.

The next day on the world news.

"Hello, I am Danielle Lockly with ABC World News. Today our first story: Tragedy in Mississippi. Two churches in a small county called Pontotoc, Mississippi, in two of their communities, Ecru and Thaxton, were assaulted by the IRS. The agents had two tactical teams with them, one for each church. Between the two attacks only an eight-year-old boy and a young infant survived.

"The people there are taking care of both until family can be reached. If you know someone who is a relative for either child, please contact the Pontotoc Mississippi Police Department. The number is below on the screen to call.

"We have one of our reporters at the Federal IRS building where the National Guard has been called out to protect those inside. We now go to John Bishop, who is outside looking at the chaos going on."

John Bishop came on screen. "Danielle, it is really chaotic here. There are a lot of angry people here wanting to know why and how this could happen. The one question that is on everyone's mind, after the past few events like this, is why are they still sending agents with tactical teams? Why would they send them to churches during prayer service?

"This crowd is very angry and is shouting church and state. Danielle, I just heard automatic weapons fire and have seen the front group fall dead. My God, they have opened fire up on the protesters! We are going to try to keep broadcasting here as long as possible. The soldiers have started moving through the crowd, and it appears they are headed for us, so we are going to try and take cover."

The video feed went out.

Danielle got as much composure as possible. As she was about to speak, the feed came back.

An injured cameraman, Eric Cannon, faced the camera. "John is dead. I managed to get away. They started shooting reporters. I, however, thanks to the Good Lord, made it thus far. I'm going to try to make it to our studios here in Washington, DC. Pray for me that I make it. There are soldiers everywhere."

Eric Cannon was running for his life in the most literal sense of the word. He had made it to the lobby of the news studio. Eric saw the guards having their weapons drawn, prepared for what was to come well as much as they could be. Before Eric could speak, a SWAT team along with about twenty cop cars filled the street. The SWAT team set themselves up outside while the police went in and took up positions in the studio.

"You need to get upstairs now. Air what you got to let the people know what is going on. Now go take the stairs!"

The guard then turned and was handed a shotgun to replace the small pistol he had drawn.

Eric ran up the stairs and into the news studio.

Upon seeing him, Danielle had a very grateful look on her face that Eric was alive.

Eric plugged in his camera to show the horrific footage of the soldiers shooting people at random. This shocked the cast and crew. Even Eric was horrified to watch it.

The silence was shattered when a gunfire was heard in the background then a huge explosion erupted downstairs.

Eric ran in front of the camera. "People, arm yourselves. The soldiers have gone crazy and are killing everyone. We here are going to leave you now. Please pray for us."

Eric took the camera with him, hoping he would still be able to transmit to show the people what was happening.

19

A New Country Is Born

EVERY PERSON IN the nation had seen the horror that had just occurred.

Small militias had armed themselves and had made calls to the local law, telling them they would defend their state and give some time for the states to pull together and form a government to fight the insanity that was happening.

Believe it or not, there were also air force militia as well. They were ready for a fight. Local towns and cities were bracing themselves for what was to come.

Morning came, and the streets were almost empty. People had barred themselves in their homes and armed themselves as much as they could.

The World News came on as the rest of the world sat in silence, wondering what to do.

"Good morning, everyone. I'm Danielle reporting to you from our West Virginia studio. Thanks to some fancy driving by our station manager, we made it here in one piece, and thanks to Eric, we have more footage to show you now. For some of you, this footage may be too graphic to watch."

Jeff was watching the news and saw the horror that had happened last night.

He offered up a prayer for all those that had lost someone and to find a peaceful solution to this problem.

As the clip ended, Danielle was handed a paper, and her eyes flew wide in shock, and she muttered, "It's about time. Ladies and gentlemen, this just in: the following states are sending representatives to Texas to discuss forming a new country, and these states are Alabama, Arkansas, Florida, Georgia, Kansas, Kentucky, Louisiana, Mississippi, Missouri, North Carolina, South Carolina, Oklahoma, Tennessee, Texas, West Virginia, Colorado, Utah, New Mexico, and Arizona. These nineteen states have decided enough is enough and are forming a new government.

"The governors of these states have activated all National Guard units to deploy along the borders of its new country called the Federation of States, and one of our sources tell us they intend on making this country a great one. Already France and England have offered itself as allies, and even China has gotten in and offered its aid in any way they can, including weapons and soldiers.

"Leaders from around the world have condemned the US for its actions against its own people, calling it a Hitler-type act. Other countries such as Canada have closed their borders and reinforced its borders with heavy troops and equipment including armored units. The press secretary had this to say: 'We are a peaceful nation and wish to have no part in America's civil war that is brewing. We have closed our borders to the states until this issue can be resolved. We will shoot anyone trying to cross into Canada at Friday midnight. Our borders will be closed, and all who wish to come here or leave here must do so by then.'

"The president of Mexico had said something to that effect as well. Most countries such as Brazil and other countries have taken a stance to close their borders to the US, for they wanted nothing to do with the situation that is developing.

"During the meeting with all the representatives from each state that wanted to become a new nation in which freedom was truly free. The meeting for the most part took little time for everyone to agree. They would now form a new country called the Federation of States. They took the original constitution and made it their own. They also made sure it was much more clear so the lawyer would not rip their constitution to shreds like the past few presidents have done to our once-great nation in which now seemed less and less like the free country had been when it was established. They had even taken off 'In God we trust' off of all of US currency."

At General Nathan Kimbel's office, he and Stacy were now discussing her promotion and her duties.

"Stacy, I'm no longer just the general of the First Texas Army. I am now First General of the Federation Military Forces as you are my second in command."

The general shifted his position in the huge office chair. It seemed too small for the man. He was very well built.

Stacy had a very concerned look on her face. "General, are you sure I'm the right person for the job? I know I have command experience, but this is a lot more than I'm used to, sir."

"You are the only person for the job. I need to know I can trust the people under my command, and you I know I can, so are you up to the task, Colonel?"

"Sir, I will do my best."

"That's all I ask."

20

Do We Really Need Allies?

"Today in World News Tonight. Russia has reunited all of its former eastern block and other breakaway nations in a cry of unity against the US for the outright slaughter of its own people. The Russians have pledged its support to be allies of the newly formed Federation.

"In other news, Russia has decided to stop calling itself the Russian Federation but has returned to the former name, the Soviet Union, and has brought back the flag of the hammer and sickle.

"China has also pledged its support to the Federation as well, and there are talks that North and South Korea both have also said they would give support to the Federation. Japan thus far has remained silent.

"Egypt is planning on engaging in talks of providing troops to aid in the fight against the US for its acts of barbarism against its own people.

"Switzerland has made itself clear this time they will not sit by while basic human rights are being taken away over money and has said it will provide troops and weapons if called on for the Federation.

"Germany has not said anything about how it will act but has been building up forces and getting ready for war, it appears, but whose side will Germany be on? No one is really sure, but they have asked all foreigners as well as the ambassador of every country to leave and not return while the world is in the mess that has recently occurred. That is all that anyone has heard from anyone in government except for one thing: a request that all German nationals return home as soon as possible. In a related story, Russia has cut all ties with the US after declaring it would support the Federation. The world is watching to see what happens here in the US concerning the inevitable civil war that is on the horizon."

For days, the White House had remained silent, and now it was nearly two weeks while weapons, food, medical aid were pouring into the Federation.

Most, if not all, of the countries have overextended their budgets and were looking at depression-type money problems.

It was now two weeks later, and the president of the United States of America had planned a worldwide announcement.

The president sat behind his desk with the seal of the country right behind him and an American flag on each side of the desk.

He adjusted his headset so people could hear him on TV and radio.

"My fellow Americans, I do not wish a war in which will divide our great nation and cause chaos through out this wonderful country. So this is what I propose to do.

"I will give each state that drops away from the Federation a one-billion-dollar tax break for all its citizens plus one billion for all education system throughout their state. All you have to do is for those states to contact us and take advantage of this chance to become economically sound."

It was not long before the phone was ringing, and Colorado was the first state to return back to the United States. And then all but Texas and Mississippi had left the Federation; however, it was only two weeks before they too gave in.

21

The Solution

"HELLO, I'M KELLY Morgan. I'm taking the place of Danielle while she is on vacation. Today on world news, the United States is whole once again. After the president made an offer, none of the states could refuse. The US has returned to its former glory, and its economic state has vastly improved since all of manufacturing has returned to US soil for the reason of supporting the Federation and starting a war machine for the United States as well.

"All material that the Federation had became a property of the state it is in, and all contracts are null and void, thus leaving most countries in a dire economic state.

"With all countries involved facing economic collapse, the US says it has a plan that will solve the global economic crises. In more simple terms of his plan, the president has decided to push forward the idea of a global currency to end multiple currency systems and have one currency for the world in which would be the global credit."

Within three days, the global credit was now the currency, and the banking system that once was was no more.

Creating a global currency led to a worldwide global government.

And so with a stroke of a pen, the world would soon be under one leadership.

So a new world constitution, and it would have far less freedoms than any of the countries had to deal with.

And all of it was done with thunderous applause.

The end.

Or is this the beginning of the end?